Collins's characterization goes a long way towards making (Ties That Bind) enjoyable.
- Steven Sawicki, *Absolute Magnitude*

The story ("Ties that Bind") is nicely written and worth reading.
- Crystal Forkan, *Tangent Online*

The ("Family Tree's") resolution (is) a pleasant surprise.
- John Everson, *Tangent*

"A Gathering of Bones" had a nice, lightly Gormenghastish streak of nastiness throughout.
- George T. Dodds, *SF Site*

I0731883

FIVE MAGICS

Short Stories

RON COLLINS

SKYFOX
PUBLISHING
Fantasy

FIVE MAGICS

Ron Collins
Copyright 2012 Ron Collins

"A Gathering of Bones" – first appeared in *Flights of Fantasy* (1999)
"Ties That Bind" – first appeared in *Adventures of Sword & Sorcery* (1998)
"The Family Tree" – first appeared in *Marion Zimmer Bradley's FANTASY Magazine* (1995)
"True Power" – first appeared in *Dragon* (1997)
"The Time of Leaving" – first appeared in *Dragon* (1995)

Cover Design: © Ron Collins

Sword Photo by Ricardo Cruz on Unsplash

Skyfox Publishing

ISBN-10: 1-946176-31-1
ISBN-13: 978-1-946176-31-8

Other Work by Ron Collins

Saga of the God-Touched Mage

Glamour of the God-Touched
Target of the Orders
Trail of the Torean
Gathering of the God-Touched
Pawn of the Planewalker
Changing of the Guard
Lord of the Freeborn
Lords of Existence

The Knight Deception

A Trevin Knight Thriller

STEALING THE SUN

STARFLIGHT
STARBURST
STARFALL
STARCLASH
STARBOUND
STARCRASH
STARGAMES

Picasso's Cat & Other Stories
Tomorrow In All the Worlds

Follow Ron at:
http://www.typosphere.com
Twitter: @roncollins13

Contents

Introduction

If I am allowed to enjoy my own work to some humble degree, the stories in this collection are some of my favorites. Having grown up reading Moorcock, Tolkein, and Leiber, fantasy has always been a guilty pleasure. The magic inherent in the genre holds an allure for me, a heady sense of expression bound in performance art. Each time the wizard stands to cast a spell, he is creating something unique, something only that mage could possibly create. In a way, each casting is then a test of the wizard's mettle. These mages and their spells are little metaphors of life that way. Each casting is its own adventure, full of inconsistencies and leading to its own joys and troubles, just as each day in our lives brings its own problems and surprises.

Thinking about it this way makes me want to live each day as if it is a magic spell, which I guess is a pretty good thing in itself.

Anyway, all of this is to say that I am, and by this time probably always will be, a fan of mages, magic, and barbaric swordsfolk of all kinds. I remember Elric, and Gandalf, and Fafhrd before there was ever the visual aid of today's movies that are so beautiful, but that also strip one of the ability to imagine things for themselves. Movies are like magic spells, after all, just as are books, and short stories. Perhaps that's why I like these stories in particular. Perhaps I think of them as my own little spells, eh? And if these five magics are spells, then that would make me...

Okay.

Let's not take this too far.

I hope you enjoy these stories, though. I've cast them the best I know how.

A Gathering of Bones

I had fallen asleep last night without making a fire, and the stone walls now stood with cold permanence in the overcast morning light. The sound of the ocean echoed inside the hollow of my room. Odors of salt and seaweed hung in the air like new ghosts. Damp fog thickened the sky outside my arched window, and waves rolled in the distance, steel-colored swells capped with streaks of white foam that broke relentlessly against the rocky beach.

I cleared my lungs with a deep breath, remembering the chore that awaited me.

My father is dead now.

The ache of his loss returned in a rush, filling me physically as if my nighttime dreams had served to keep this reality away. He had been working in our open-air laboratory, concocting another spell that he would someday pass on to me if he found time. Something went wrong. The explosion rattled the whole of Castle Talon, the small stone building my father and I have lived in for as long as I can remember.

He probably never knew what happened.

Fitting. My father had always been a man whose focus was intense, who could set aside distractions in order to concentrate on what he found important. And as one of the distractions he oftentimes placed aside, I knew how firm the walls around those compartments had been.

So today I was alone inside this place he named after the hawks, the place where the two of us have lived for so long, alone to deal with him like I have always been.

And for the last time, deal with him I will.

I tightened the drawstring on my trousers and slipped my summer sandals onto my feet. The morning was cool and overcast, but the sun would soon burn through the morning mist. Building Father's pyre would be hot work, and there was no one else here to share the labor.

Kiva chose that moment to land heavily on my stone windowsill. Her golden brown feathers beat against the air as she navigated the tight quarters. Once settled, she stood proudly on the sill and stared at me with her intent black eyes, her gaze unwavering but nervous, the feathers of her chest ruffled and full.

At her feet lay a bone, the small curved rib of perhaps a mouse, bare and smooth, its surface gray in the morning gloam.

Her call pierced the room.

"Fly, Kiva," I said while making a sweep of my flat hand, the motion that meant she should return whence she came.

But she did not. Instead she cocked her head and continued to stare intently at me.

Confused and angry, I strode to the windowsill. The sound of the ocean was stronger here. The wind blew cold against my face, moving my dark hair away from my eyes. The bone lay pitched up at one end. I twisted it around in my fingertips. It was dry and brittle, its surface slightly roughened like the finest of all sandpaper.

But it was just a bone.

I let it drop outside the window, knowing it would be lost amid the shale rock that lined the beach.

Kiva called again, and she leapt off the sill, swooping downward to catch the bone in midair just before it disappeared into the jagged rock. In a moment she had perched back on my windowsill and the bone lay again in its spot.

"Damnation," I said to myself, wondering if she had lost the common sense that the gods gave all creatures. "All right, Kiva. I'll keep it." I slipped the bone into a small pouch that was clipped to my belt, then turned and walked out the door.

I had more things to worry about than a deranged hawk.

For as long as I can remember, we have kept hawks at Castle Talon. As of this past breeding season there are fifty-eight of them. We leave them free to come and go as they please.

And yet, they stay.

They always stay.

My father studied them intently, casting sorcery amidst them on more occasions than I could possibly count. They fascinated him, and drew every ounce of his attention. While he loved them all, he had been particularly fond of Lissa, a huge hawk with golden feathers and a wingspan as large as my father was tall. He doted over her, speaking to her in quiet moments, and watching her glide over the land, flying majestically in the blue sky while he remained locked to the ground.

His eyes would mist sometimes.

And after these times he would increase his efforts in the laboratory, feverishly studying magic and incantations at the expense of his own physical health.

He wanted to get closer to the hawks, I know. He wanted a deeper connection.

I remember a night in a distant tavern where father and I had traveled to fill a contract for his sorcery. Father, as he always did, had brought Lissa with him. A woman with thick, red lips and wearing strings of gold so false that even a boy my age could see them for such, asked if I was jealous of the birds.

I didn't know what to say then.

Certainly I was jealous. I knew *that* to the core of my being. I never understood my father's single-minded fixation on these creatures while I stayed outside his circle of concern. But at the same time, the hawks were as much a part of my life as they were of my father's. I fed them in the winters. I cleaned after them as they needed cleaning after, and I tended their wounds and sicknesses as they arose.

The hawks were a part of my life, and if truth is told, I had in some ephemeral fashion always felt attached to them. I asked my father about them once, though.

"Why do we have so many hawks?" I said.

His face grew troubled and distant, and he pursed his lips. For just an instant, his eyes softened, losing the edge that his glance always carried when he looked at me. He tried to speak, then stopped. He breathed deeply and hesitated longer.

"You will understand when you are older."

Father's smoke was gray and black. It curled upward in thick streams that twisted like drunken snakes and smelled of driftwood and salt. The hawks, all of them, glided in the sky above, riding drafts and twirling downward in a dance that seemed almost ritualistic.

The fire baked my face and prickled my bare chest with heat that made my skin ache. Sweat I had given in the preparation of the pyre boiled away.

When the burning was done, I cast a spell over the embers. Fire can hide, and no matter the castle's dilapidated condition I had no intention of waking to find my newly inherited manor burned to the ground. It was an easy spell, among the first my father had taught me.

I sighed, watching the last of the flames snuffed.

When my father was alive, there was always a goal—always a plan, a new spell to try, or a fresh experiment to run.

But he was gone now. And yet I felt his presence stronger than ever before. His gaze seemed to come from each direction, expectation riding upon it as thick as the morning mist. The familiar hills reminded me of him; he had been like these hills to me, always here. How could they still spread from the oceanfront and he be gone? I thought of the creases in his forehead that I, too, would likely have someday, and he seemed even more real. I turned to the castle, expecting at any moment that he would step from the laboratory doorway and announce he had discovered some new facet of his magic.

He was not there, of course.

I had watched his body burn and the smoke that carried his soul waft up into the hawk-filled sky.

Now I felt like a lifeboat cut free from a ship, adrift and loose on a windless sea.

Drained and hungry, I returned to the castle.

Kiva swooped down to land gracefully on a perch beside the doorway. Another bone slipped from her hooked beak, falling to the ground at my feet. She called again and stared at me insistently. I picked it up. This bone was similar to the last, but a bit larger.

It was certainly not from a mouse.

Kiva had been borne of Lissa, as had been the rest of the hawks that wheeled in the air above. But Kiva had been the first. She stood in much the same way as her mother had, held her head in a similar fashion and moved on a perch likewise. Strange, I thought. Or perhaps appropriate. Lissa had died a fortnight ago, sending my father into the laboratory for his last feverishly pitched efforts at developing new magics.

Now both Lissa and my father were dead. And it was Kiva, Lissa's first daughter, who brought me these gifts.

My muscles ached from my day's efforts. My stomach growled and my thoughts wandered. Without questioning her this time, I slipped the bone into my pouch with the other.

Given a hawk's eyesight, nothing alive can move so

much as a hair's breadth in the territory around Castle Talon without the knowledge of one of our—my—birds. So it was no surprise when several days later, the hawks roused my attention.

Men were coming.

As always, I set the precautionary wardings, magical traps that would protect me if I needed to retreat into the castle. Men had often come here seeking sorcery, and my father was nothing if not cautious.

Nervous energy played inside me as I waited. This was the first time I would handle business on my own, and I worried about the encounter. I used the time to play conversations in my head until the words became a jumbled mess that was more confusing than helpful.

Five men arrived an hour later, riding horses that jangled with metal and leather harnesses, and whose hooves beat heavy patterns on the earth. The men wore brown and dark green. They carried weapons, but not in any outwardly aggressive fashion. I stood before them in tanned breeches and a billowing blue tunic. Leather talon guards were strapped around both of my forearms, their rawhide cords tied with comfortable pressure.

Hawks glided through the air above me.

"We've come to see your father," the leader said. He was a rugged man with sun-blond hair and a face chiseled from years on the trail.

"He is dead," I answered, the words coming oddly to my lips.

"That's damned unfortunate," the leader replied.

I ignored his comment. "I am Cullen. I run Castle Talon now. My father passed what he knew to me. If you require the aid of a sorcerer, I will listen to your situation."

The leader considered my statement, confusion written on his face. "I am Parr, from Ellingsworth," he finally said. "The king's daughter has taken a sudden illness, and he has need of a sorcerer's aid."

I could not help but frown. My father had been born in, and had lived in, Ellingsworth for many years before my birth. Yet while men from all across the continent had from time to time come to barter for my father's sorcery, none had ever arrived from that city. And now, scant days after my father's passing, here stood five riders asking me to travel to that place with them.

"Ellingsworth has a strong clergy. Isn't such a problem better handled by them?" I asked.

Parr's face darkened. "King's already tried that. The high priest prayed for days but nothing worked. Now the church says she's been cursed by sorcery too strong for them to break."

Lines crossed his face. He was anxious dealing with sorcery, as many are. It was a prejudice my father suffered often in his life. Sorcery is wild and confusing to people who do not understand it. It is powerful beyond their ability to comprehend.

"I will go to Ellingsworth with you," I said. "Assuming the price is acceptable."

"Princess Terisa is the king's only daughter," Parr said angrily. "The queen died years ago. Rest assured he'll pay you more than you're worth."

I snorted, surprised at this man's bluntness. "Fair enough. I'll travel with you. But let me tell you I don't take kindly to such pointed comments, and <u>you</u> can rest assured that an upset sorcerer will cost your king more than a comfortable one will."

Wheeling in the sky, Kiva called and swooped down. I held out my arm, and she landed lightly on it.

"We are going on a trip, Kiva."

The men looked at her, obviously distrustful of the bird and uncertain of its tie to me.

"Tell the others," I said, motioning her to the sky once again.

She took to the air then, calling loudly with high-pitched screams. The rest of the hawks flew around her, responding and gliding out over the prairie that stretched away from the rolling ocean.

The men remained quiet, but I could see the display had done nothing to reduce my stature in their eyes.

My father had taught me well.

I offered to put the men up overnight in Castle Talon, but they decided to make a campground in the hills to the east, explaining that they had not been near the ocean before and wanted to be in the open while they were here.

I smiled and pretended to accept their words, all the while sensing their anxiety.

So I slept alone in the castle, the physical separation of the men from Ellingsworth speaking volumes, telling me that I was not like them, that I was dangerous.

I suppose I could not help but dream about my father. As the night passed around me, I asked him questions that he would not answer. I requested advice he would not give. Despite these rebuffs, or perhaps because of them, the conversation felt warm and familiar. His voice rumbled and his breathing rasped nasally like it always had. When the beam of his concentration would fall fully on me, he was gentle and easy to talk to, a natural teacher with a calm demeanor and a lighthearted approach.

I woke fresh and oddly confident, feeling close to my father, a sensation that fought with my ingrained fears and doubts to make a mixture of emotions that was not completely pleasurable.

By the time we left, Kiva had placed three more bones on my windowsill—one a round vertebra the size of a pea, one the curved needle of a ribcage, and the other a small pelvic segment. I placed each into my pouch, still no further along in puzzling out why she was leaving them.

But my collection had now grown to a firm handful.

The city was large and sprawling. It smelled of baked bread and fried meats.

Buildings of white stone and yellowed brick towered over the landscape. A large river ran past to the east, glittering with the silver-gold reflection of the setting sun as we entered the main gates. Men pulled carts through rutted streets. Women carried ceramic bowls and woven baskets on their shoulders. I caught a whiff of cinnamon, and my stomach growled.

Parr had no time for my hunger, however, and directed us toward the king's castle.

This was the city my father had grown up in. I stared at it as we moved, dwelling over the buildings, imagining him as a boy playing tag or kicking rocks, and wondering with each moment if he had ever stood in the exact spot where I was now.

I glanced at Kiva.

She rode anxiously on my arm. At first I attributed her demeanor to her distaste for the city's closed space. But as we progressed she grew more agitated, ruffling her feathers and stretching her wings often. A hawk's silhouette graced the sky above, another of our birds following at a cautious distance.

I had never previously known any of the birds to follow my father and me when we traveled, and the novelty of its appearance in conjunction with Kiva's odd discomfort made me feel uneasy.

As we neared the king's castle, the gates opened and an armored guard approached.

"How is the princess?" Parr said as he slid from his mount.

The guard grunted and pulled at his well-trimmed beard. "Worse off, from what I hear," he said gruffly, his expression grave.

Parr gave a deflated sigh. "The king?" he asked.

"With the princess."

"Come on," Parr said to me. "There is no time to spare."

I swung my leg over my horse's saddle, glad for the opportunity to stretch my muscles.

The guard pointed at Kiva. "We can put the bird in the aviary," he said.

Kiva had not calmed any, and I would not leave her alone for fear of adding to her anxiety.

"Thank you," I responded. "But I will keep her with me."

The guard glanced at Kiva, then looked to Parr with a question in his gaze.

Parr merely shrugged and motioned me to follow him.

"It's all right," I cooed as I went, noting Kiva's heightened nervousness with each of my steps and hoping my assertion was correct.

Kiva opened her wingspan, then settled in a little.

We walked across the manor yard. It was a large, rolling field that seemed to absorb sound. Crows strutted across the green grass, scattering as I drew near, their shoulders shimmering with blue-sheened lurching motions. The fragrance of corn and beans and tomatoes came from the king's garden.

Members of the manor stopped as we passed them by. The weight of their awkward stares burned on my back. I felt the presence of my father then, so close I could smell the faint bitter reek of sorcery that had always hung around him. I had watched him handle this situation time and time again, walking into a place where people around him feared what he was, feared the whole of what he stood for.

In an unusual burst of verbosity, he had talked to me once about it.

"You must go into a new city as if you own it, Cullen. Or else it will own you."

Remembering his words, I threw back my shoulders and set my face with the same firm countenance that had once been his. We are very similar in features, my father and I. I know this. And now I cast myself as him, twenty years younger and walking into Ellingsworth with all the confidence in the world.

A doorman opened the gates.

We entered the castle, our footsteps muffled by plush rugs that lined the floor. Clean-burning candles lit the expansive hallway of gray stone. Paintings and heavy tapestries lined the walls. Kiva grew suddenly subdued.

"Come," Parr said anxiously.

He led me through the hallway and up a set of wide, sweeping stairs. A long corridor led past several doors before we stopped at a guarded chamber.

Nurses stood anxiously around the bed. The king sat in an upholstered chair by the princess's side, his eyes worn and hollow, ringed by dark circles. Age had lined his face and tinted his hair with gray streaks. He wore simple, unkingly clothes—a yellow tunic and cloth breeches. But he held himself with the firm posture of someone accustomed to obedience.

"Parr," he said, rising.

"The mage was dead," Parr said quickly, not taking the care to soften his language for me. "So I brought his son."

The king stepped before me, glancing once at Kiva with a strange expression of dread. His eyes took me in from top to bottom, his face an odd mixture of hardness and pain, and something else, too, something seething underneath, angry and cold but hidden under layers of restraint.

He did not <u>want</u> a sorcerer here, yet had asked for one.

"You are your father's boy. No mistaking that," he said with a sword's edge to his voice.

"Thank you," I said, trying not to furrow my brow. My father had never mentioned his association with the king before, which, of course, was so like him as to not need thought. "Let me see the princess," I continued, trying to divert the conversation into a place more comfortable.

He escorted me to her side.

I placed Kiva onto the sill of the open window by the bed, then bent to examine the princess. Kiva opened her beak as if to call out, but then settled into place, staring now at the princess with intense concentration.

Terisa was dark, like her father. Her face, however, was gaunt and sickly; her skin pulled over cheekbones like dry leather. She was about my age, I saw, maybe a year or two older.

I placed my hand over her forehead and spoke a quick magic. Her body radiated the pale crimson light that only sorcerers can see. Her form glowed through the sheets with cold magic that echoed through my mind.

At my side, Kiva spread her wings and gave a shrill screech, a sound that reverberated with a yearning for freedom so universal as to be unmistakable.

My eyes narrowed.

Burning heat grew against my thigh. I looked down to find light radiating from my pouch. This glow was blue, however, and it met with the crimson sorcery over Princess Terisa to bathe the room in lavender and black shadows.

The bones, I thought, this new magic sprang from the bones Kiva had been laying at my feet since the day my father had died.

Kiva called out again, and urgency came to my spell work.

Something new grew inside me, burrowing out of my understanding like a rodent emerging from the ground. The birds have magic, I thought, remembering my father's words when I had asked of the hawks' presence.

Sorcery whirled around Kiva, and she fed my spell with magic of her own. I felt her heartbeat swishing rapidly through her body. I saw into the magical realm of my spell work with the clarity of her vision. And what I saw shook me.

The link that enveloped us grew, closing a loop that included the princess. The three of us—Kiva, the princess, and I—were all linked, bonded in some fashion seemingly inseparable, and that bond *was*, in some way, my magic.

"What is it?" the king asked breathlessly.

Ignoring his question, I bent further over the princess. Yes, her complexion was dark like her father's. And she had the severe curve of his nose. But the shape of her face was familiar, rounded at the cheekbone and tapering at the jawline. Her hair had bronze highlights.

Similar features to those I saw every time I looked into the reflection of my father's mirror.

Kiva called, a shrill scream that made everyone in the chamber jump.

"Get the damned bird out of here," the king said.

The guard moved toward her.

"No!" I called. "Kiva must stay."

She stood in the open window, her wings partially unfurled, their curve graceful and fluid. Her heartbeat still fluttered against mine, and her gaze was still intense. Magic flowed from her. Another heartbeat joined ours then, slow and methodical, so familiar it could have been my own.

The princess.

With that sound, with the throbbing beat of Terisa's heart so very much like my own, I knew the truth with such startling clarity I found it hard to breathe.

I clutched the bedclothes and turned my gaze to the king. Blood drained from my face.

"She is my sister," I said accusingly.

The king looked crestfallen. "Yes," he admitted, his head nodding almost absently.

The gasp from those in the room was audible.

"But my father?"

"Was once my own wizard," the king said. His eyes grew sharp and he set his jaw. "I sent him away."

"But only after I was born and it became obvious who my father was," I said, making it a statement rather than a question.

Kiva cried again as if prodding the king. For an instant I pondered the power of her magic, the sway she might hold over him as well as over me. But there was not time enough to consider this fully.

"Yes," the king finally said, speaking as much to Kiva as to me. "I was angry. I was jealous and embarrassed. So I sent him away, and I sent your mother, the queen, away, too."

"But, sir," Parr broke in. "The queen died with her stillborn son. The entire land mourned her for months."

Movement stopped in the room. The king chewed his bottom lip. Kiva spread her wings farther and stared into the king's gaze.

The king shook his head. "No, Parr. Lissa did not die."

Lissa.

The name rolled off the king's lips and rang through my head with a peal as clear as a church bell. Lissa. Lissa. The name of the queen. The name of the hawk my father had kept beside him his entire life. Lissa. Lissa.

The link between the princess and Kiva and me still burned. I thought for a moment, knowing now with certainty that just as Terisa and I were siblings, so, too, somehow were Kiva and I.

"She became a hawk," I said in a stupefied monotone. "My mother, the queen. She was a hawk."

The king nearly broke down. Tears formed in his eyes. "Yes. She had always kept a raptor in the castle, and it was her falconry that drew your father and her together. So I felt it fitting punishment. I paid dearly for the spell that made her a hawk and tied his magic to her soul. Then I sent them away."

The king drew a chest-wracked breath.

"But now my daughter is dying, and I don't know why. Please save her. She is all I have left."

Fire burned along the top of my thigh. The pouch glowed with blue waves.

The bones.

I touched their magic flame and felt what I for the first time in my life knew to be my mother. She was warm and she was kind. Through her eyes I saw my father, their awkward early meetings, the love that grew between them that both fought against, and the fervor with which he had worked in his later years.

He had spent his life trying to free her, but the binding had been too great.

And with both of their deaths, the bond had passed to her next generation—including her daughters, Terisa and Kiva. Kiva and I were together throughout the past weeks, but Terisa was alone. And bound as we were, none of us could live apart.

But the magic was weak, now. I could feel it, see the cracks in its casting.

And I could break it if I wanted to.

If I wanted to.

I shuddered with the thought.

"You will understand when you are older," my father had said. And now I did. The king had tied my father's magic to the hawks. I knew this to be true. All of my magic was founded on the birds, fueled by their existence and the link I had to them.

If I broke this binding, I would no longer have magic of my own.

The thought rang in my heart and sent ice through my veins. I had been raised since a boy to be a sorcerer. I knew nothing else. The truth of the moment sat before me like a starved lioness.

Terisa lay on her bed. She had been apart from us for too long. If I did not cast the final spell, she would die. Kiva folded her wings and sat calmly on the sill, awaiting my decision. She, too, was caught in this web of deceit spun by the king and queen and their wizard. If I did not cast the final spell, we would be bound for the rest of our lives.

And if I did cast the final spell, I would lose my sorcery, the only thing my father had left me.

The king looked at me with deep, watery eyes.

He had lost his wife and his friend years ago. When news of his deceit was released, he would likely lose his rule. And now he stood to lose his daughter no matter what I did.

Outside the window, the sky was dark with circling hawks.

I reached into the pouch and withdrew the bones of my mother. They were weightless, shimmering with magical heat. I clasped my fingers around them, holding on to her for a moment that seemed to last forever and to be gone at the same time.

She smelled of orchids, my mother.

And her smile was playful.

The spell came to me unbidden, the words flowing easily, the fullness of courage and justice expanding my chest and making my heart feel as if it would burst.

This was the right thing to do.

I cast the bones down on my half sister's bed, speaking the final phrases of the spell work.

"Will you stay?" my sister said to me with pleading eyes.

She had recovered rapidly, and now we sat on a pair of iron lounges in the king's gardens, perhaps like our mother and my father once had. A light wind blew dogwood and apple tree scents from the west.

I wanted to stay. That I could not deny. We had much in common, having both grown up without a mother.

And I wanted to know my sister. There was procedure to follow, but her father was stepping down from his rule and soon she would be queen. I wanted to see her grow through this moment in her life.

But I shook my head instead. "No," I said. "I have a whole life to discover again, Terisa. And I'm not ready to stay here. I will return, though."

She smiled. "I understand. This is your home, though. Do *you* understand?"

I matched her smile and nodded. "Yes," I said. "This is my home." And suddenly it was. I felt it in the way Terisa smiled, and at the way we had grown comfortable with each other's presence in such rapid fashion.

We stood then, and I gave her a hug.

Terisa smelled of orchids, and I of my now dead sorcery.

"Will you go back to Castle Talon?" she asked.

I stared into the birdless sky. The hawks had left after the spell had been cast, scattering into the hills and the mountains to live in the high rock as all hawks should. Even Kiva had left. I had given them back to the gods, who they rightfully belonged to. I was alone now, truly alone.

"No. I'll travel for a while. Father used to tell me of his wanderings as a boy. Perhaps I'll follow his path."

"Good luck," she said with a playful smile. "I'll

look forward to your return."

"As will I," I replied. "As will I."

I left the next morning.

The king offered me a horse, but I decided I wanted to walk. I felt like a weeks-dry sponge, empty and waiting. I wanted to know the land and see it up close. And the closer I was to the ground, the more real it would be, the more I would learn from it.

I strode alone past Ellingsworth's tall buildings and out of the main gates. The soil smelled of clay. The grass had the cold edge of the approaching fall season. I set off to the east, toward the Ridge Mountains.

The sun rose higher in the sky, and the day became warm. I eventually stopped to make my lunch.

My father was a good man. I knew that now. He loved my mother, and she loved him. He was caught up in his magic, and he was caught up in his efforts to find his love. Maybe that was enough for me to forgive his lack of attention.

I planned to think about it often in the next weeks.

A shadow flashed silently over the sun-drenched grass.

I glanced up at the same time Kiva called out.

Her feathers golden brown in the sunlight, she

swooped down from the sky, gliding on unseen currents to land on a branch above me.

She sat silently, her magic now as dead as my own. Her glance was nervous and self-conscious, or perhaps I was just applying my own understanding to her actions. The other birds were gone, their tie to Castle Talon rent with the tearing of my inheritance. Kiva and I were no longer bonded by sorcery.

But I felt close to her in a way stronger than ever before, and I think somewhere deep inside her eyes I saw this same connection. I reached to my side and pulled out the pouch of our mother's bones.

They were still there, light as air. Kiva watched me, her curved beak seeming to cut into the afternoon.

I untied the drawstrings and emptied the pouch onto the ground before me. The bones fell, crumbling at the touch of soil, spreading and melting into the earth as if they were made of water. A whiff of orchids twisted in the breeze, then it was gone.

Kiva cried a mournful sound, full of sadness and emptiness, yet carrying undertones of understanding. I had been born of two human beings. Kiva had been born of my mother's body and my father's magic.

Now the souls of both had been joined.

Their lives were done.

Ours was about to begin.

I stood up, wiping my lips with the back of my hand. "You're welcome to travel with me, sister," I said to Kiva, strapping a leather guard over my forearm.

And Kiva, bound to me in a different fashion than I had ever felt before, flew to my hand.

Ties That Bind

Elron of Keth stood over the Black Knight's prostrate form. His breath came in deep gasps that tasted of blood and sweat and the grit of the gladiator Circle. His ears rang with his pulse.

The knight's eyes narrowed into dark balls of hate. He glanced from Elron to the edge of his blade. "Do you have the courage to finish?" the knight said with superiority that didn't match his position on the dust choked field.

Elron grimaced and gripped his sword in both hands. A single stroke and the knight was silenced forever.

At first the only sounds were the pounding of Elron's heart and the wind whistling over the field. Then a throaty roar broke through like the rhythmic throb of a charger galloping closer through a foggy mist. He stared into the stadium seats. People shouted and gestured, their faces red and their mouths moving. Guardsmen stood outside the Circle with armor that gleamed in the midday sun. Kallus sat behind the wall, a smug smile affixed on his heavily jowled face. The man next to him threw coins into Kallus's lap and rose angrily to leave.

He had done it. He, Elron of Keth, was the new Champion of the Circle.

Elron lay on the wooden tabletop and tried to relax. Steam from the master bath filtered through the spa's ductwork to hang in the air, its jasmine scented heat making Elron's lungs hurt. On either side a young woman rubbed him down with liniment made from a mixture of mint and animal oils.

Kallus lumbered into the room and slowly lowered himself onto a bench along the wall. Steam washed over him, and a film of sweat immediately formed over his blubbery belly, running to pool in the creases that formed in his gut. He was short man, too big around for the towel he wore. The cloth strained to its fullest as he leaned forward.

"Excellent show today," he said.

Elron peered through one eye. "I hope you found it profitable."

Kallus smiled contently. "Indeed. Everyone wants a piece of you, now, Elron. You are a celebrity."

Silence.

Kallus had assigned himself as Elron's agent

over a year ago when Elron had been captured during a Tawntorian raid on Keth. While their agreement had saved Elron from an early death in the mines and provided him access to finery better even than his station in Keth had, he had no false conceptions of kindness on Kallus's part. Elron was still a slave, no matter that his chains were made of sorcery rather than iron.

"I see your wounds have been tended to," Kallus said.

"As always. I'm sure I'll be ready for your next assignment within a fortnight," Elron replied.

"That won't be good enough this time."

Elron raised his head off the table and arched his back, propping himself gingerly on his elbows. Sweat from his brow ran down his face. "What do you mean?"

"You fight again in three days."

Elron laughed. His thigh was bruised and tender, and his left elbow had swelled to twice its normal size before the healer applied his magic to it. His calf muscle still ached. No matter how powerful the magic, it seemed the body only healed so quickly.

"I've fought for you for over a year, now. You know me well enough to trust my word. I'll never be ready that soon."

Kallus stood and padded over to him, his fleshy feet slapping against the damp stone floor. "And you know me well enough to realize I don't care.

You're the Champion now, Elron. There's good money to be made. You'll be ready when I say you are."

Elron stared into Kallus's face and saw determination. A thin tingle crawled down Elron's back, reminding him of their linkage—the agreement they had made.

"As if I have any choice."

"There is that," Kallus replied, smiling wickedly. He ran a meaty hand over the backside of one of the women. "I'll leave you in good hands. With help like this, I'm sure you'll have a speedy recovery."

Elron glanced at the woman to his left. She was certainly attractive. But all he could see were blue eyes that reminded him of Marian. And all he could feel in her touch was the way Marian used to knead his muscles after he'd spent a long day over his smithy fire.

Kallus waddled out of the chamber, and Elron lay down again, closing his eyes and resting his head on crossed arms while the women silently rubbed knots from his muscles.

The sorceress rolled her head backward and groaned, a sound of ecstasy tinged with something dark and evil. Her black hair was streaked with gray, and her face was lined in fine wrinkles. Her dark purple robes shimmered with a violet sheen in the light of the three flickering candles.

Elron stood before her, coarse hemp biting into his wrists and the rags he wore doing little to fight the chill that suddenly sprang up inside the hut. Unpleasant vibrations from her magic washed over him. His hair seemed to dance on his scalp, and his flesh crawled.

When she was finished, she stared at him, obviously drained from her exertions. Her eyes, golden irised and wide, were filled with concern. "You are a good man," she said in a hoarse voice. "I can tell."

She moved toward him with fragile steps, as if balancing on a tree limb. She placed a dry hand on his chest, its skin rough against his. The silver ring around her forefinger gleamed. She leaned against him, bringing her sorceress's lips closer to his ear. "This spell cannot be broken while Kallus lives," she whispered. "You cannot destroy him, nor will you be able to leave his employ."

Then she was gone, leaving behind the ghostly smell of damp straw smoldering on an open fire.

Elron woke in a cold sweat, despite the spa's heat. The dream returned to him after every match. The link defined his life. It could be worse, he supposed. Kallus left him free to attend banquets and other publicity opportunities, and people always wanted to be seen with a rising star of the

Circle.

He would have even more attention now.

But it was a hollow life compared to the one he once had. It was not his own. He had no place to call home, no place where he fit with the rest of his world. Before the raid, he had been respected as Keth's finest blacksmith. Friends stopped by his place everyday to share stories and talk about events around the city.

Before the raid he had Marian.

He thought of her. How soft her hands felt as they brushed his brow, how she smelled of springtime, how her lips had tasted of wild strawberries when the two of them had lain in the open meadow.

And he saw her dragged away by Tawntorian guards as they marched prisoners to the slaver camps.

Elron had never seen her again.

Now he was alone, bound to Kallus by a sorceress's link.

He raised himself painfully to a sitting position, the towel that had been draped over his backside falling to the floor. He made no attempt to retrieve it. The women had left some time ago, so there was no reason for modesty.

Three days.

He flexed his arms and felt their complaints.

He would never be ready in three days.

Elron straddled the fallen man, towering over him, his shadow falling across the man's body. His opponent stared up into the sun, shading his eyes weakly with the palm of his hand.

This time, Elron heard the crowd.

Their cheers and shouts swelled inside his head, their excitement boiling in his blood. He smelled his opponent's fear. The man struggled to crawl away, clawing at the dirt and leaving a bloody trail.

Elron raised his mallet, concentrating to ensure he finished this battle in one stroke. The muscles in his arms burned with the strain of lifting the heavy weapon.

The man gasped. His eyes glazed over, and he spoke to himself. "I'm finally coming to see you, Mother."

Elron paused and, for the first time, actually looked at his opponent. The man was a pitiful match for him. Small and weak. His armor ill fit him, and he had no skill with the blade he carried. A sure victim from the minute he stepped into the Circle. A crimson river flowed from the man's nose. One arm bent at an awkward angle. Elron was certain he had broken several of the man's ribs with a mallet blow a moment earlier.

Elron lowered the weapon.

The crowd murmured, confused at this development and frustrated at the unsatisfying lack of blood.

"Where are you from?" Elron asked.

The man stared back at him, dazzled from either the sun or his pain.

"I said, where are you from?" Elron kicked him a glancing blow—more for the crowd's sake than anything else. After a year in the Circle, he had learned how to play to an audience.

The crowd roared, demanding blood.

"Davensfort," the man finally responded, his voice thick and wet with blood. "My family is there."

Elron placed his mallet head on the ground beside the man's head. "Family?"

The man's lips quivered as he spoke, his gaze darting between Elron and the mallet. "My wife. Three boys."

This was no gladiator. Not even a slave. This man was a father and a husband. He likely worked the fields to feed citizens of this city. Elron was suddenly embarrassed he had not noticed this earlier, so intent was he at the start of the match. "Why...?" Then he knew. Taxes. The king had recently needed money to pay for his daughter's wedding. Citizens were angry over the new rates.

It was not an anger that a slave like Elron had to worry about.

"This is your punishment for being unable to pay taxes?"

The man nodded, his focus drifting again.

Elron tossed the mallet away and walked with a steady gait toward the box where Kallus and the other contest administrators sat. The box was behind the Circle wall, a short barrier of cut stone no taller than Elron's waist. Their faces were firmly set, and their glances full of questions. Kallus's cheeks reddened with rage.

The crowd hissed and booed.

"Finish it," Kallus shouted.

Elron shook his head and stopped five paces from the wall. "I agreed to your arrangement. But I'll not kill such an opponent."

"Your link binds you, Elron. Go finish your task."

"No, Kallus. My link is silent now. I agreed to fight gladiators, not farmers. I am within my right." With that, Elron turned and left the Circle, exiting purposefully through the tunnel leading into the spa.

Kallus was still dressed in his daytime robes when he entered the chamber this time. His jaw was clenched, and wisps of short, graying hair stuck out in the humidity. His jowls shook with every step, and his eyes were aflame with anger.

Elron closed his eyes and leaned his head against the wall, pretending that Kallus could be ignored. The healer had not yet made his visit–not that Elron really needed his efforts after this day's battle. The stone's heat soaked through him, and the image of his opponent's gaze bore in on him.

The sound of Kallus's footsteps halted in front of Elron.

"That was quite a display you put on out there. What were you trying to do?"

Elron opened his eyes. "That man had no cause to die."

"That is not yours to decide, Elron. Yours is to do as you're told." Kallus shook with anger.

"What is your concern, Kallus?" Elron said. "We won. Your prize money is safe and sound. Why are you so upset that this poor creature didn't bleed more than he had to?"

Kallus leaned over to put his face before Elron's. His lips curled downward, and spittle flew as he spoke in terse sentences. "You're obviously too damned stupid to comprehend what's going on here! You're the champion, Elron. You don't make money just for me anymore. There are people who run this world, people far stronger than the king, people who kill with the twitch of a finger."

He straightened and drew a deep breath, regaining his composure. "But to ensure you understand this situation, Elron, I'm going spell it out to you." Kallus put his arms behind him and paced. "That man was there for a reason, Elron. You're the champion. You face a string of losers from here out. Your record builds. In four months no one will remember who you've beaten. In fact, these puny bags of dung you've destroyed will take on larger proportions as time marches on—it's human nature, Elron. And when you've gotten a large enough stature, a reputation of invincibility, you take on the next up-and-coming champion—who's been groomed for the same stature."

Confusion buzzed inside Elron. He had become accustomed to the fact of his slavery. He lived for Kallus's livelihood. He stepped into the Circle and fought for his life with other men, winning glory or suffering death. But suddenly the sand had shifted, and Elron felt uncertain of his position, violated and used beyond his endurance.

"So I'm to kill a person every few days so you make even more money later."

Kallus nodded. "You've got over thirty victories now, Elron. At this rate, you'll be approaching seventy by midsummer. Then you'll be ready."

Elron's heart beat in his chest. Anger flared. He remembered his match with the Black Knight. The Champion had fatigued more quickly than Elron had expected. "I'll be worn out is what I'll be. I'll be no match for my challenger."

"That would be a sad ending to your saga, Elron. A sad ending indeed. But if it comes to pass, your adoring spectators will carry warm memories of you in their hearts. A better end than many get, I'm afraid. Much better than the ending that poor man in the Circle has achieved today, I'm certain."

Elron frowned. "What do you mean?"

Kallus patted his knee condescendingly. "It shouldn't bother you one bit, Elron. You did what was in your heart, I'm sure. But your show of pity merely made those people I spoke of earlier very angry. Your challenger was executed in public shame shortly after you left the Circle. Just as every man you leave standing from here on out will be."

A chill spread over Elron's skin. His thoughts jumbled. Despite his best efforts the man had died and been publicly humiliated in the process. Heat rose to his face, his blood scrubbing his veins raw with anger. Elron glared at Kallus. The grubby fat man stood there smiling with evil indulgence, his eyes glittering as if laughing at Elron's predicament.

Control slipped away from Elron. Kallus's presence grew within him. The smell of oblivion. The wheeze of his breathing carried overindulgence and evil pettiness. The expression of fear on the face of the man in the Circle flashed in Elron's mind, clouding his vision. It was more than he could bear.

Kallus must die.

Elron rose, towering over Kallus and reaching toward him with his muscled hands. Kallus stepped backward, but Elron's fingers still coiled around the man's neck.

Pain.

A lightning strike inside Elron's chest.

He doubled over and fell to the floor, every muscle clenched, his face contorted in agony.

Kallus's voice rasped through the curtain of pain. "You belong to me. Your link ensures it."

The pressure lessened inside Elron's chest, and he opened his eyes again. Kallus was blurred through tears.

"But believe me, Elron. I'll not tolerate another outbreak like this. "The fat man smoothed his robes, smiling wickedly. The healer arrived, carrying his bag of ointments and various wrappings.

"I'll leave you to your medicines, Elron."

Elron was tired. His muscles ached from months of the Circle. The faces of men he had killed flashed in his memory. Round faces, wet with sweat and blood. Angular faces with screams etched in their eyes. The face of a man who fought as if he were a demon on fire, then seemed almost to welcome the death Elron brought to him.

The sharp smell of ointment and burning wood filtered through the room. Women rubbed Elron's muscles, making small talk about his body and dropping innuendo as to what he might be able to do with it when the match was over.

Outside, Elron heard tension in the spectators' voices. The preliminary battles were completed.

Rising stars had dispatched their opponents, and the entertainment between bouts had finished. The feature would start in moments. The Champion would finally fight the Challenger.

But inside the dressing chamber Elron found it impossible to concentrate on anything but his tired bones and the faces of dead men.

Kallus stepped into the room, and the women parted. He walked carefully to Elron's side and patted him on the shoulder, smelling of stale wine and cheap perfumes. Elron's business had been lucrative over the past months. "Good luck, my friend," he said. "This is the real test. The day your reputation is made."

Elron stared at his agent with vacant despair, feeling the bitter strength of the link that tied him to the fat man. He wanted to be angry at Kallus. He wanted to hate and despise the man. But instead of hate he found pity. And rather than despise him, Elron found himself truly astonished at the deep sense of sorrow he felt for the empty place that must surely reside inside the man's heart.

Standing, he hefted a heavy sword and held it in the same fashion he once held his smithy's hammer, absentmindedly testing its weight and balance.

Without a word, Elron stepped into the tunnel leading to the Circle. His footsteps echoed in the corridor's hollowness, a resonance Elron compared to the sound of Kallus's heart beating inside his soul. His chest was bare, and the chill air raised bumps on his skin. Leather plates strapped to his thighs made soft creaking noises as he walked. His hair had grown long in the past months, and he tied it back with a blue cloth. Blue like the color of Marian's eyes. Blue like the sky under which they had last touched.

Who was he now? He had once had Marian. He had once been proud of himself. He had once had people who cared for him.

Now he had nothing.

At his entrance, an excited buzz crackled through the gathering, rapidly building to a loud cheer. Elron's body was sculpted, covered in muscle honed from months in the Circle and shining with oils that gleamed in the bright summer sunlight. His followers were delirious, urging him on and smelling blood.

That the Champion came unannounced indicated he meant business. That he wore little armor and carried but a single weapon surely meant he was prepared to destroy the Challenger rapidly—the ultimate in confidence.

He rested his sword against the Circle wall and used a handful of dirt to dry his hands, wiping them on his loincloth.

A thin man stepped out and shouted at the crowd. "The Circle announces the Challenger to the Champion, Dakeed 'The Reaver'."

The crowd roared.

The Challenger strode behind his entourage, his agent and his handlers. The man was as big as Elron, perhaps larger. He wore leather armor over much of his body and a beaten bronze breastplate that showed scars of previous battles. A curved sword hung at one side, and a heavy dagger was strapped to the other, its well-honed edged glittering in the sunlight.

Elron stood with arms crossed as the Challenger finished his preparations. Their gazes locked. Dakeed's eyes were tight and focused, concentrated beads of icy blue. As his preparations neared their end, the Challenger's handlers walked away, joining Kallus in the open pavilion behind the wall.

The crowd stood, their presence heavy yet ephemeral, loitering outside the Circle like a ghost at a funeral. They roared their approval when Elron left his weapon at the wall and stepped into the circle for the formality of the center greeting.

The Challenger met him there, and they shook arms, Elron grasping Dakeed's forearm as firmly as the Challenger did his. Hot sun beat down upon the two, and sweat broke upon their brows to run down oil-slicked foreheads.

"Why are you here?" Elron asked him.

The Challenger glared at him.

Elron continued. "I am here because I will die otherwise. I am here because my handler must pay for his wine."

"Don't play games with me, Champion. I have seen you slice your way through rows of counterfeit soldiers. Have you enjoyed paying for your agent's wine with the blood of farmers?"

The comment stung, and for a moment Elron could not speak. His expression must have shown his hurt, for the Challenger appeared confused.

"I hope you never have to find how it feels firsthand," Elron finally said. Then he returned to the wall to pick up his sword. The crowd sensed his anger and erupted in a bloodthirsty cheer.

The two combatants met in the center of the Circle amid the clang of steel upon steel. Elron's weapon was heavier but not as quick. He sidestepped to avoid the Challenger's dagger and swung his own sword behind his head, bringing it back to an attack position.

The Circle drew its veil around them, and Elron no longer heard the crowd or smelled their presence. Only the two of them existed now.

No, that was wrong. Elron felt another presence, one that would always be there, tingling at the base of his spine forever. The sorcerous link between him and Kallus was omnipresent, lingering like an itch under his skin.

The Challenger feinted, and Elron stepped back, blocking the attack with a wave of his blade. Though it was early in the match, Elron's arms and wrists already burned with fatigue.

The Challenger pressed forward, missing with a sword thrust but slashing at Elron's leg with his dagger and drawing a thin line of blood. He paid for his boldness, however. Elron caught the Challenger off balance and tripped him. Dakeed landed heavily in the dust and only a quick roll to his left saved him from being skewered on Elron's sword point.

They circled each other warily, both realizing that each was more skilled than their previous opponents, both coming to grips with the understanding that only one of them would walk out of the Circle.

Elron swung his sword and drove the Challenger back, buying a few moments' breathing time.

They skirmished again. This time Elron emerged with a stream of crimson running from his upper arm, and Dakeed lost one of the pads protecting his thighs. Elron breathed heavily, his muscles aching. Sweat rolled off his body, smelling of brine and tasting of salt.

"Why did you choose that weapon?" Dakeed asked as he circled Elron. "It is too heavy for a long match."

"Perhaps I intend to kill you quickly."

The Challenger swiped at him ineffectually with his curved sword. "Or perhaps you mean to die slowly?"

Elron slipped away from Dakeed's sudden

charge, unsuccessfully trying to trip him again. Dakeed was right, he realized. Elron would not last long with the heavy sword. Perhaps, he thought, he did want to die. Had he enough of living life tied to one who thought of him as merely a source of his next meal?

The link burned in Elron's mind. It twisted through him as if Dakeed had planted his dagger in his kidneys and turned it. If he died here, at least the link would be gone. Perhaps, he thought, if he were going to die anyway....

The Challenger attacked, driving the Champion backward. Elron slipped and fell to the ground, his sword landing a distance away from him. Dakeed slashed at his legs and fell on him, trying to drive his sword into Elron's skull.

Elron slipped the attack but was pinned under Dakeed's weight. He grabbed his opponent's wrists and held them firmly. They struggled, neither of them able to force movement in the other.

Finally, Elron spoke through gritted teeth. "Perhaps you are correct, Dakeed. Maybe I do wish to die. So let me offer you my crown in return for a favor."

"You are in no position to ask for anything." Sweat dripped from Dakeed's face, and his breath was hot against Elron's cheek.

"Grant me my sword that I might kill my agent before you claim your victory."

Dakeed hesitated, and Elron was able to throw

his weight to one side and scramble away. Dakeed stared strangely at Elron as the Champion crawled to his feet.

Elron's sword lay at the Challenger's feet.

Dakeed slowly sheathed his own sword and bent to pick up Elron's. The crowd's bloodlust rose, seeping into Elron's world for the first time since the match began.

"You are linked?" Dakeed said to Elron with surprise. It was a statement as much as a question. He closed in on the Champion.

Elron crouched and moved stealthily backward, keeping himself ready for the Challenger's next attack. His link sizzled with the strong smell of sulfur. He needed his sword back, he knew. Without it, he could not kill Kallus. "I said I was here because I would otherwise be dead."

Dakeed glanced into the crowd. "My link burns also."

Elron followed Dakeed's glance to the box where Kallus sat with the Challenger's agent, both obviously enjoying the bout.

"You cannot kill him, either?" Elron asked, a light dawning.

The Challenger swung the Champion's sword. Elron leapt back again, nearing the stone wall.

Dakeed shook his heed. "No. I cannot kill him."

They stared at each other in a new light. They were brothers of a sort. Both tied to those who would use them. Neither able to live as they wished.

"But you can," Dakeed said.

Elron smiled. Yes. He could kill Dakeed's agent. And Dakeed could kill his. An even swap. He glanced hurriedly around the coliseum. Excited spectators shouted and screamed, waiting for blood and death. Kallus sat stoically, wearing the expression he wore when he talked of money.

Guards, armed with blades and covered with armor that shone in the sun, stood at various points around the Circle.

"We'll never leave the Circle alive," Elron said.

The Challenger slashed at the Champion, a wild arcing blow that had little chance of landing. A rabid surge of enthusiasm boiled from the spectators. Dakeed, too, knew how to work a crowd.

"Better to die together than alone," Dakeed replied between breaths.

Elron ran his hand through his hair, his fingers brushing against his headband. He remembered Marian and saw her blue eyes through the haze of dust. His jaw set. Marian would be embarrassed of the life he was living.

... Better to die together than alone ...

Elron nodded and stared at Dakeed as he slowly retreated closer to the wall. He reached back and felt its rough surface, realizing he now stood only a few steps from the Challenger's agent. "Together," he said through his constricted throat.

With his spare hand Dakeed drew his dagger and flipped it in the air, catching it by its point. The crowd roared, their bloodlust at its peak after watching the Champion be backed to the wall. He tossed Elron's sword vertically, leaving it hanging in the air for the Champion to grab. In the same motion, Dakeed threw the dagger.

The weapon whirled through the air, its edge flashing before burying itself in Kallus's chest. Elron grabbed his weapon and spun on his heel, neatly severing the neck of Dakeed's agent.

There was a sudden hush from the crowd, and everything halted. Elron and Dakeed immediately dashed toward the tunnel. Elron quickly dispatched the first guard. Dakeed ran beside him, drawing his own sword.

The two of them fought in tandem, blades flashing in the sun. Blood splattered. Screams of pain rang out. Elron's muscles screamed with fatigue at each slash, and his breathing came hard. But the link was gone. He was free, and adrenaline coursed through him, bringing him raw energy to carry on.

From the corner of his eye, Elron saw Dakeed take down a guardsman and fend off the attack of another. An armored swordsman came upon Dakeed from behind, and Elron buried his sword into the guard's back, saving his newfound friend. Dakeed glanced at Elron as they fought, respect in his expression that Elron hadn't seen since his days in Keth.

He was cut, and blood flowed from his leg as strongly as it flowed from his shoulder.

But Elron felt no pain.

He drove his blade into the gut of the last guard standing between him and the dressing chamber and ran forward, Dakeed hobbling along behind him. More guards would be outside. But Elron was surprised to find the guards didn't worry him. It did not matter whether he and Dakeed escaped or not, he realized.

The itch of the link was gone, and instead of pain or anger his heart soared with the lightness of being that came from freedom and the closeness that came of brotherhood.

He paused at the door to the exit passage and looked at Dakeed.

The Challenger was gone, and in his place was a young man who was struggling to be free also.

"Come, Dakeed," Elron said, clutching his sword. "Dying together would be fine. But it would be better to live!"

Dakeed smiled, his eyes softening for an instant before he brandished his own blade. The sound of armored soldiers echoed from the other sideof the doorway.

Elron put his shoulder to the door and pushed.

The Family Tree

"We are dying, and I shall be the first to go." Ryl sat at her root and shivered. She grimaced with each frail movement, and the other women offered her words of comfort.

Lyra's voice rose above them. "It is Gorduin. He must be stopped."

"How? We cannot leave the forest for long enough to confront him," Ryl replied.

"One of us has yet to be linked to her tree."

There was a hushed gasp among the women.

"You mean your daughter?" Ryl finally said.

"Yes. I suggest I leave and bring Kerna here. She is the only one of us who can stand against Gorduin."

"But you will die if you leave your tree."

"If I gather all of our magic, it should sustain me long enough to return with her."

The night grew into the women's silence. Crickets and cicadas played their evening symphony and the call of a nocturnal animal accentuated the moment.

"She is but sixteen; her tree is not yet ready," Ryl said.

"Yes, she is young."

"She is our future."

"Again, correct. But, I can think of no alternative."

There was a murmur among the women. Their magic would not be easily given. But Gorduin was descended from the wizard whose curse had tied them to their trees; they would not take his threat lightly.

Finally, Ryl spoke for the grove.

"Take the magic. We will die either way."

Kerna loved it when her father played his music. It meant the day had gone well. It meant food in her stomach and a warm fire in the hearth. It meant they would not spend the evening brooding over where her mother had gone or why, two years ago, she had left them.

He played an old oaken reed, one that had been her grandfather's, and his father's before that. Dark spots stained the oakwood; smooth rings the size of silver coins were worn into the finger grips and tone holes. Kerna planted herself on a soft pillow, laid her head on crossed arms, and let their fire's warmth seep through her. Her muscles relaxed and ridded themselves of the leaden load that accompanied every evening. A sound invaded her luxury, a sound so quiet that, at first, she almost missed it. But her father stopped playing and the sudden silence exposed the soft squeak of the door's inward swing.

Kerna turned her head and opened her eyes. Standing at the door was a robed figure – short and slight. Kerna strained to see further, but the evening's darkness hid any additional features until the figure stepped forward. The robe was deep green and tied at the waist with a heavy belt made of coarse, woven hemp. A hood cloaked their intruder's face.

"Begone ye, wizard!" her father said as he stood to defend them.

The figure's hands slowly rose. They were fine hands, soft and clean. They closed on the hood, seeming to caress the material as they pulled it back.

Kerna gasped.

Her father stopped in mid-stride.

"Lyra?"

"Yes."

Her mother had returned. Kerna's heart beat against her chest and blood burned in her cheeks. A shiver ran down her spine. Her life could go back to normal. She would do her daily chores and help her mother ready the evening meal; nights would be time to play and listen to her father's music. Then the shiver of joy became a spasm. Why had she gone? She looked beautiful, slim; her hair was thick and full, her face unscarred and smooth. She did not look at all like she had weathered a hard escape from anywhere. Had she really abandoned Kerna, like the other girls whispered? A cold wind blew through the open door, making Kerna's skin goosebump. Red and brown leaves skittered across the earthen floor as her mother reached for the door and swung it shut.

"What are you doing here?" her father said.

"I'm sorry, there is no time for pleasantries. Kerna must come with me." She held out her arm to Kerna, her hand palm-up and her fingers curled into a gentle beckon. Kerna felt a sudden attachment, a completeness as if a hollow spot in her chest had suddenly filled.

"You can't have her."

"Don't fight this, Jonah. It is important."

"No. This is not going to happen to me again."

Lyra's face softened and her eyes took on depth. She smiled lightly.

"Kerna will have a final call, but this is not it. This is something different."

Kerna stood and faced her mother.

"I'll go," she said.

"No, Kerna." Her father's face had a firm set but he made no attempt to block her. The fire light combined with age to draw deep curves over his cheeks and encircle his eyes with half-moon-shaped arcs.

Kerna felt her mother's contact from across the room. An overpowering aroma of spicy perfume and fresh-cut wood stung her nose. Kerna walked toward her and took her hand. Her mother's skin was silky and moist; her firm grip enclosed Kerna's hand and drew her closer. The folds of the green robe wrapped around her. The room grew fuzzy and the floor melted away.

The undergrowth crunched beneath Kerna's feet and the hoots and howls of night creatures reached her ears. The smell of fresh pine rode on the gentle night breeze. Kerna and her mother stood in a small clearing amidst a forest that filtered the light of the full moon so that she could scarcely determine much else about her surroundings.

She looked at her mother.

"Is it really you?"

"Yes."

"Why did it take you so long to come back to us?"

Kerna's mother held both of her hands and knelt on one knee, allowing Kerna to tower over her.

"I am so sorry. You cannot know how much I miss you and your father."

"Then why did you leave us?"

Her mother's grip moved to Kerna's upper arms.

"What has your father told you about me? About us?"

"Father speaks only of your leaving."

Her mother was silent. Kerna's eyes adjusted to the darkness and she saw moonlight glisten from her mother's tear-streaked cheek. Leaves rustled. The cry of a bird of prey resonated through the trees.

Finally, her mother spoke.

"I did not wish to leave you. But we are cursed, Kerna.

I had no choice."

Kerna's silence prompted her mother further.

"You are a dryad. Do you know what that is?"

Kerna gazed warily at her mother.

"A nymph, a wood faerie," her mother continued.

The words ran through her head but didn't quite register. Of course, she knew of wood faeries. Her friends told stories about faerie magic and beautiful women who were half-tree and half-human. But, this made no sense.

"How...?" was all that Kerna could muster as a reply.

"I am a dryad, too. As was my mother, and hers."

The world spun under Kerna's feet. Was she dreaming?

"What is this curse?" she finally said.

Her mother looked up at her with wide eyes

that reflected the moonlight. "Centuries ago, one of our ancestors was to be wed to a powerful warlock. She chose to elope with a common woodsman instead. The wizard was so enraged that he placed this curse.

"Each of our line finds true love in a human mate, just as I did with your father. It is a love that is greater than any you can imagine. We bear a single daughter, as I bore you. When she is born, a tree sprouts in our grove, as did one at your birth and at mine. And, when that tree is ready to accept a permanent resident, we are called to it. Our true loves are unable to follow and we are tied to our trees, consigned to live our lives separated from them."

Kerna's mother sighed deeply and pointed to the small tree that stood directly in front of them. "This is your tree," her mother said.

Kerna stepped closer to examine it. While it was no sapling, it was young; she could easily have encircled the trunk with her arms. Kerna reached out and touched it.

Leaves rustled with her contact, a soft, gentle hiss that she found comforting.

She looked at her mother's face. There was pride and dignity in her eyes – and a sorrow hidden somewhere deep underneath them.

"You told father that it was not my time. Why am I here?"

Kerna's mother grimaced. "Look closely – tell

me what you see."

Kerna peered through the darkness. At first, in the moonlight, they all appeared to be normal, sturdy oaks. But eventually she began to notice things. Patches of mold or fungus grew on many of the trunks; branches drooped and sagged; leaves had holes eaten through them. The sight disturbed her.

"What is it?" she finally asked.

"The whole forest is dying."

"Why?"

"Gorduin, a descendent of the wizard who cast our curse, is draining minerals and nutrients from the ground. We are slowly starving to death."

Kerna contemplated the statement.

"How can I help?"

Her mother turned to stare directly into Kerna's eyes.

"Our trees hold our magic; we want you to enter our trees

and take this magic. Then you must go face Gorduin."

They took each other's hands and stood in silence, listening to the night's noise. The forest wrapped itself around her – the smell of dried wood, a screech owl's cry of victory, the creaks and groans of trees moving in the wind. Her mother's hands were warm. Kerna felt the synchronized beat of their hearts and felt her mother's love for her and for her father.

"How do I enter the trees?"

Kerna struggled up a rocky hillside toward Gorduin's castle. The building was made of mortared stone and brick, and adorned with wooden doors and shutters. A thin trail of smoke rose from a chimney and dispersed into the early morning overcast.

Her body tingled and the hair on her arms and legs stood on end. Individual dryad magic was not strong, but in the collective it was substantial. Kerna hoped it would be enough. There were trees in the area to cover most of her approach, and she easily made it to the huge door without being seen. She ran her fingers over the wood. It was dead, stained and sealed with oil. But it was still wood, and her magic was strong. She spoke gently to the door, begging its forgiveness and preparing it for her assault.

Once she felt it was ready, Kerna stepped through the door. It felt just like stepping into her family's trees, a pleasant sensation, a feeling that the top layer of her skin was being gently scrubbed.

The castle was smaller on the inside than she had imagined. Cramped and cold, the hallway was made of yellow brick, and was lit by small tallow lamps that burned from within wall sconces. Kerna slipped through the hall without a sound.

At its end she found a narrow staircase that led upward. She followed it and entered a small room that opened to an outdoor platform. Soft noises could be heard emanating from the area, scratches and the low tones of a male voice. Kerna approached the doorway with slow, even steps.

She eased her head around the open doorway.

Kerna almost gasped. The balcony was huge and opened to a dramatic view of the canyon behind the castle. Plant life of all kinds covered a majority of the floor space. She crouched low and picked a slow path toward the sounds. Finally, she was able to peer through a broad-leafed fern and see Gorduin.

He was younger than she had expected, probably no older than twenty – and thin, but not so spindly as to appear weak. His long, straw-colored hair hung loosely around his shoulders and Kerna could see his features were fair. The blue of his morning robe blended with the gray of the platform's stone to give the illusion that he was a carved statue rather than a living human.

Kerna was astonished to see that Gorduin was holding an open palm toward a small, gray squirrel – feeding the creature crushed nuts and cooing softly as he did it. The image was in stark contrast to the one she had envisioned. She shook her head – these thoughts must be avoided. She was here to save her family, and Gorduin was their murderer.

Kerna moved through the foliage and approached Gorduin from behind. Her movements were, again, silent, her breathing controlled. She aligned her thoughts and began to channel her new-found magic toward her heart as her mother had taught her. She drew to within arm's reach before the squirrel gave a high-pitched squeal and scurried away; its fright made Gorduin look up, and his astonishment was easily visible.

"What —"

Kerna touched his shoulder and funneled all the magic she could through her body. She felt power in its release, power that she could have never imagined. Her mind went blank. All she knew was the feeling of golden tendrils surging from her fingers and into Gorduin, searching for his essence, yearning to snuff it out.

There it was. She felt his soul and held his life in her hands. In an instant, her family would be saved.

Then she felt Gorduin's response. Their magic clashed with golden and blue sparks, exploding with such force as to throw the two apart. Kerna was shocked by the collision. But she was more shocked by what she had felt when her dryad magic had held his soul. She looked across to the corner where the explosion had thrown Gorduin. His head had hit the wall, and blood oozed thickly from a wicked gash. His face went suddenly ashen.

Kerna spoke. "There is nothing but good inside

of you. Why are you killing my family?"

"I am sorry – but I am trying to end this curse." His voice trailed off as if his attention waned.

"But your family is the one who placed it – only my family has been damaged by it."

"Not true. Ever since that curse has been laid, we have undergone terrible misfortune. My brother was killed by marauding thieves, my father fell victim to a terrible disease, my grandfather...." A deep coughing fit interrupted his thought. "My grandfather was killed in a landslide. It goes on through my entire lineage. I wanted to stop the curse so that my future children may live full lives."

Kerna sat in silence. She looked closely at Gorduin. His eyes were dilated and his skin was porcelain white. She stood and strode quickly to his side. Her hand went to his forehead and she felt beads of clammy sweat. Gorduin started to raise his hand, then dropped it again to his side.

"Do not worry." Gorduin's voice was a rasped whisper. "I am the last of my family. The magic that drains the dryad's forest will die with me. Your family is saved."

His eyes rolled upwards and he became unconscious.

"Perhaps, there is another way to break this curse," Kerna whispered.

She held his head between her hands and focused her energy again. Again, dryad magic flowed from her to him as she searched for Gorduin's essence. And, once again, she found it.

It was broken.

She wrapped her tendrils around Gorduin. But this time, she did not seek to extinguish his spirit. Instead, she searched deep into her own soul and found warmth and energy.

She channeled it through their linkage, pouring more and more of herself into him.

When she was spent, she withdrew and waited.

Kerna sat by the nighttime fire and rocked the cradle that held her sleeping granddaughter.

"Mother?"

"Yes, Celene," Kerna replied.

"Is little Lyra all right? It is getting cold. Is she covered?"

"Yes," Kerna said, her face breaking into wide creases as she smiled. The babe was fine, but her daughter's question reminded Kerna of the coming winter. She wrapped her shawl tighter around herself.

A deep breath rattled through her lungs. She thought of another night, so many years ago when her own mother had returned. The thought reminded her of the forest – of the tree that held her mother and of her father's grave lying at its foot, of her own tree, waiting for her to take up residence, of the trees of Celene and little Lyra.

Those trees would no longer call them away from their true loves, but would always be ready.

Kerna looked up and watched Celene finish the evening dishes. A smile crept to her face as she remembered her daughter's expression when she had been introduced to her dryad family.

Music started – the thin song of an old reed with age-stained spots, worn finger grips, and smooth tone holes.

Kerna's gaze left her granddaughter and moved to the other side of the fireplace.

There was Gorduin. He was aged – stooped by the years and scarred by wrinkles and deep lines. He held her father's reed in his hands and, with his eyes closed, played the melody.

She watched him sway gently with the music, and she hummed softly in accompaniment. She hummed for the years they had lived together, and for the love that had broken the curse that once stained both of their houses. And, even after all these years, she hummed for the warmth he brought to her heart.

The love she felt for him was greater than any she could ever imagine.

True Power

"Teldrin, the time has come for you to develop your true power." Attruic-eb spoke in a low, coarse voice. A bronze brazier smoldered at the center of the table, its embers glowing, reeking sourly and casting an eerie pale on Attruic-eb's wrinkled face and graying beard.

Teldrin forced his heart to calm and hoped the smile he felt rising to his lips was not too visible. His gaze met that of Attruic-eb. Despite his age, the elder wizard's eyes glittered.

"I am honored, Lord Superior."

"I'm sure honor has nothing to do with it," Attruic-eb replied. "For months I have watched you place barriers in your opposition's path, deliberately impeding my other apprentices and using their failures as stepping stones for your own advancement." He paused. "It has been...entertaining."

"It was you who taught me the advantages of proper preparation, Lord Superior."

"Apparently I have taught you well."

An awkward silence hung for several moments during which Teldrin could hear only the hiss of burning embers. He stood before Attruic-eb's throne-like chair and stared at his own feet. This was it. Three years of work was about to come to its conclusion. "How do I do that, Lord Superior? How do I develop my true power?"

"Do not be coy with me, mageling. I am aware you have spent considerable time studying the order's bylaws. You understand there is only so much power in this world. In order to claim your own, another's must be freed."

"What is your will, Lord Superior? For I am also aware that only a master can cast the spell that triggers my talent. You hold the key to my progress. What duty am I to be assigned before you will make me a wizard?"

Attruic-eb tilted his head back and stared down his nose at Teldrin. "I have discovered the whereabouts of a ring of power. If you bring it to me, I will grant you status."

"What is this ring?"

The Lord Superior smirked. "Some magics are too strong to be tampered with by one of your experience. Suffice to say its retrieval will ensure you a healthy start toward your mastery."

"Where is it?"

Attruic-eb brought his hands together and rested his chin upon his fingertips. "On the hand of a Lectodinian mage."

Teldrin contemplated this situation for a moment. Lectodinian activity was always at odds with Koradictine, but direct confrontation was usually to be avoided–wars between the Orders were often bloody. "So I must steal it."

"Obtain it however you will. But I seriously doubt you can take it while the mage lives."

Teldrin peered into Attruic-eb's eyes, trying to discern a hint of humor but finding none. "Surely, you do not mean that my power-task includes killing a man."

"Of course not," Attruic-eb replied, enunciating each word with the sharpness normally reserved for berating poor performance. "The Lectodinian mage who wears this ring is a woman named Raevyn."

"Such an action will surely spark a war."

"Is this actually what concerns you, Teldrin? Or are you merely hiding a fear of killing?"

Teldrin thought on this. He let his stare wander to the brazier and lose itself in the embers that lay smoldering there. He would steal for power, there was no doubt about that. He would cheat, maim, lie–whatever it took. And he would kill. He was surprised at this realization, at how easily the decision had come. There really was no decision.

It had always been there–the fact that he would take another's life to lift himself to a position of power, to dominate a piece of the world. It had been there since his father had governed their hometown of Twillen, proving himself to be weak and unwilling to take advantage of his position, wasting the opportunity to wrest control for himself when it was there for the taking.

"Obviously, I will require aid to defeat an established sorceress."

Attruic-eb nodded. "Place your dagger on the table."

Teldrin did. The blade had been his father's, an offering from the leader of a neighboring village. He almost grimaced, remembering how his father refused to use the blade to broaden his control. How sweet, he thought, that a symbol of his father's weakness would serve to establish Teldrin's own true power.

Attruic-eb's fingers shook slightly as he held them over the blade. He spoke a few words of magic, and his fingertips glowed. A luminescent pink mist enveloped the dagger, bringing a gleam to its edge.

Finally, Attruic-eb looked at Teldrin. "The dagger will provide you defense against magical protections. Use it well. It should give you entrance to Raevyn's lair."

"I am ready, Lord Superior. I will let nothing stand between me and the power that is rightfully mine."

Attruic-eb sat back in his chair. "I never doubted you would."

The ring on Raevyn's finger grew warm. She turned her gaze away from the volume she was reading and stared at her hand.

Someone is asking about us, my dear.

The voice was familiar, gentle and seductive with a silent edge that should have warned of danger back when it was not too late, but instead had lured her deeper into its clutches.

"Yes," she said out loud.

Excellent...it has been too long since we last had a caller.

Raevyn stood up and walked to a floor-length mirror. She brushed hair from her face and stared into hollow eyes. Familiar anxiety washed over her–fresh longing mixed with dread. Her stomach churned with an odd mix of questions. Was he a good man? Would she siphon his vitality slowly, feeding her own sorcery and watching him wither as his life seeped away? Or would she take him quickly and see the morbid shock on his face? Did he have family?

How long could she continue like this?

Don't get sentimental again.

"Be quiet, please. I need to be alone."

But, Raevyn. You will never be alone. I am yours, and I am always here for you. Together, you and I are invincible. A perfect pair, bonded for eternity. Just like you always dreamed.

Raevyn's jaw clenched. Yes, she had always been afraid of being alone.

She sighed and stared deeper into the mirror. Men's faces flashed at her. Ten. Fifty. A hundred. Who could remember through the centuries? Kayelwyn, pure and powerful—she had nearly smothered on the intensity of his energy. Fraydon, who had almost lived through their encounter. Danlim, the Prince from Tawntor, who had stolen her heart, but who had suffered more from her curse than any of the others. Everyone she touched was dead by her hand.

It was tiring, this life. And trying. She might live forever. She performed any magic she desired. But what good was immortality if all she could see were faces of men she had killed? What good was unlimited ability when there was no one to share it with?

She gazed forlornly around the chamber. Candlelight flickered, illuminating velvet-covered furniture and marble sculpture. A flowing fountain gurgled in the distant corner. Paintings of open landscapes adorned the walls, seemingly lifeless in the dim shadows.

Raevyn thought about the man who would soon arrive. She wondered what his dreams were, and she was saddened to know he would never achieve them. Perhaps he wouldn't come. Perhaps he could resist temptation. But Raevyn knew better than to put credence to these hopes. The ring would find a way to provide for her.

It always did.

* * * * *

Teldrin stood in the midnight shadows of the moonless night, tucked into the darkest corner of a back alley, waiting for a man named Varga to appear, a small-time thief and big-time snitch. If anyone knew where Raevyn's hideaway could be found, it would be someone like this.

The night air was cool and wet. Teldrin leaned against a decrepit tavern made of mudbrick and rough lumber. A coarse scent leaked through cracks in the walls, seeping into the streets to be carried off by a slow breeze. Inside were mostly addicts and gamblers, men who smelled of garbage and who spoke their guttural language in whispers that sounded like rats scampering through sewer drains. Teldrin despised them. They were weak, and without vision—the lowest form of life.

He had been in Daggertooth for three long days. It was a small town, a prospecting city built on mountain gold and filled with pickpockets and murderers—all of them spineless, afraid to talk about a lone sorceress. Teldrin touched the handle of his dagger and smiled. Before he could steal the ring, he had to know Raevyn's exact location. What money apparently could not buy in this town, the blade would surely discover.

Varga stepped out of the tavern. He was short and thin, scrawny, with greasy hair pulled back by a knotted headband. He walked down the alley toward Teldrin's position, swaying slightly with each stride.

Teldrin waited. Once Varga passed him, Teldrin stepped forward, wrapped his arm around Varga's chest. The thief struggled for a moment, but calmed considerably when Teldrin held the dagger against his neck. "We need to talk," Teldrin said, "and I won't take no for an answer."

Varga hesitated, considering the situation. "Then I won't give it," he replied at last. His breath was fetid.

"I'm looking for a woman."

"Aren't we all," Varga snorted.

"Where can I find Raevyn?"

"You're talking to the wrong man."

Teldrin applied more pressure to the dagger. "This blade carries my magic, Varga. I would almost enjoy testing its edge this evening."

Varga grunted, a sarcastic sound—almost a laugh. "You are a fool if you think a simple piece of enchanted steel will protect you from Raevyn."

Teldrin said nothing, merely increased pressure upon the blade. Blood beaded at the weapon's edge, and a thin dark line ran down Varga's neck.

Varga's voice dropped to a whisper. "She lives in the mountains, halfway up the north face of Hammond's Peak. Look for three rocks that sit atop each other, and follow the mountain up another hundred paces. There, you will find the opening to her cave. But, I'm serious. There's no quicker way to die than to tangle with this sorceress."

Teldrin grinned. The home of a feared sorceress should have a grander entranceway. This would be easier than he thought. "I am no schoolboy," Teldrin said with more confidence than necessary. He pulled the dagger away from Varga as he pushed the thief farther into the alley's shadows.

Varga collected himself and peered through the darkness, as if studying Teldrin's face. "You are a fool. Raevyn has lived in these parts for as long as most can remember. She comes to town now and then. And every time she comes, men die. Listen to me. You're best served leaving Raevyn alone. She devours souls. She'll use what you give her, and she'll take what you don't."

Teldrin merely nodded his head and walked away. Suddenly, he stopped and turned back to Varga. "Thank you for the advice. I'll remember it when I rule this land."

Teldrin spat, and continued up the road.

All that Raevyn ever really wanted was to be loved. At least that's what she had thought when she was a child.

But that was before magic entered her life, before she felt electric energy dance along her arms and before she brought a flower to life. That was before the ring.

It had promised to fulfill her dreams.

And it did. Once she slipped it on her finger, she became the person she always wanted to be.

Awkward as a girl, Raevyn grew beautiful as she aged. Shy at first, she began to draw men without effort. As each relationship flourished, the ring fed her with sorcerous power that was stronger than any before. These men would stay with her for varying periods of time—weeks, or even months. But eventually she would become bored with each man, or they would slip away.

As her stature grew, she drew more attention. And with each champion, her sorcery became even greater.

She should have known where the power was coming from. Perhaps, somewhere inside her mind, she really had known but was afraid to face the truth.

Once she finally understood that her growing powers came at the expense of these men, that they were left hollow and lifeless—eventually dying— once she understood this horror, it was too late. Like a haggard drunkard who curses life's unfair evils as he buys another tankard, Raevyn was addicted—willing to do anything.

She realized she was nothing more than a slave, and would be for the rest of her life.

Teldrin slipped the pack off his shoulder. It had

taken him a full day to get here—three rocks, formed atop one another.

He was unused to walking in altitude. His muscles ached. His lungs screamed for a full breath. A thin sheen of sweat covered his forehead, bringing a cool sting from the mountain air. He looked over his shoulder and watched as the sun edged closer to the horizon.

The thin air carried the heavy aroma of fresh pine—and another odor also, one that perhaps only Teldrin could sense. Power. Energy. It was here, ready for the taking.

Rested, Teldrin hefted his pack to his shoulder. He breathed deeply, and he strode farther up the mountain.

He came upon an opening, a simple cave more than anything else. He paused to withdraw his father's dagger. The blade glowed pink. Holding the weapon before him, he entered, walking softly. The cave was damp and smelled of mildew. The cavern grew dark, the dagger's thin gleam was all that lit his way.

The walls were rough-hewn, scarred by the picks and chisels that had gouged out the passage. The floor sloped upward and curved back upon itself, making a slowly spiraling helix. There was no sound. Teldrin moved as if in a dream. The walls became smooth and unblemished, a texture that no craftsman could achieve alone.

He paused.

What power could carve these walls? How would he manage to steal such power from its wielder? His heart pounded, the cave's stillness making the rush of blood throb in his ears. He shook his head to clear these thoughts. Self-doubt would ruin his quest. He would be victorious. He had to. There was no other possibility.

With a final shake of the head, Teldrin began walking, progressing unheeded until he came to a door.

Raevyn sat on her couch and stared into the water-filled bowl on the table before her, watching as the young man climbed the path to her door.

He draws nearer, my love. Are we prepared?

What would this one bring? Would he be sweet and tender? Or would he be primal and instinctive—like so many of the others—direct and bold in his questioning but limited in his ability to understand the answers?

The ring grew warm on her finger and blazed in Raevyn's mind. It tugged and pulled at her soul. Fresh energy. Power. It is ours. Take it. Let it flow through you. He wants you, Raevyn—like all the rest. It is right that he be ours.

Raevyn struggled against these urges only briefly. She had tried to fight them before, but found the effort futile. The ring always won, and the more she fought, the greater sorrow she felt later.

Teldrin paused before the door. It was carved from oak and inset with silver sigils and oddly asymmetrical glyphs. His muscles quivered as he pressed against the door, his throat suddenly dry. Power was behind this door. His power. He sensed this in a fashion that he could never describe, an aura that hung invisibly in the air, a surety that this was his destiny.

Gripping his dagger, Teldrin pushed gently. The door moved. Swirling fragrances filled his senses. Jasmine, patchouli, clover, persimmon—the odors came and went, but there was no breeze as he slipped through the doorway.

"You won't need the blade," a feminine voice said.

Teldrin looked toward the voice. Raevyn lay seductively on her couch, her long hair falling darkly around her face—black with subtle highlights of reddish brown. Her skin was smooth, with gently curving cheekbones and full lips. She wore a dark dress, midnight blue with silver lace at the waist and high-collared throat.

At first, Teldrin thought she was beautiful. Then he stared into her eyes. There was pain and darkness in them, anxiety and internal struggle, a harsh reality that burned through him.

He straightened. "Perhaps I won't," he said,

annoyed at having lost the element of surprise so early in the encounter. Teldrin slipped the dagger into its sheath, but kept his hand in close proximity.

Raevyn's lips quivered. Energy crackled in the space between them.

Suddenly she was standing before him, so close her breath moistened his face. Her aroma engulfed him, fresh and vital, the scent of a mountain waterfall. She leaned forward and their lips met.

Her power scorched his mouth. Her kiss tasted tangy and wicked, dangerous. Energy and emotions mixed inside his mind, flowing through his body, seeping outward as if the force of Raevyn's kiss pulled upon them. By the time he realized his hands could no longer reach his dagger he no longer cared.

Raevyn stood over her visitor as he slept. His face was slim, its muscles relaxed in slumber. She ran a finger along his cheek. It was smooth and tender. How long would he last? How long before this cheek would be cold and stiff? How long before she would take him to the burying place in the heart of the mountain?

Raevyn grew warm and her thoughts jumbled.

Come, my love, while his energy rages. It is time to prepare new magics.

Raevyn nodded her head silently and turned

away.

Teldrin awoke to find himself on a large, down mattress covered with blue and pink silk sheets. He gazed around the room, peering through half-lidded eyes that felt swollen and bloated. A tallow candle sputtered on a stand across the room. His robe was thrown across a chair. His dagger lay on the ground. He tried to remember why he was here. He tried to remember where here was. But his mind was hazy, his thoughts hollow and slow to come. His head hurt.

He slid off the bed and was surprised to see he was naked. Then he remembered Raevyn, the bed, and sensations he had never thought possible. The ring.

The last thought brought some reason to his senses. He stood and slipped into his robes. Sliding his dagger into his belt, Teldrin looked around. Darkness and confusion limited his ability to see far, but a door-shaped area of blackness stood out across the room.

He went to it, and soon found himself peering down a long hall. Golden light came from an open doorway. Teldrin thought he heard a voice, lyrical and steady. But it was so soft, and so thin, he couldn't be sure.

As he drew closer to the doorway, the air grew charged and thick. The floor was cold against his bare feet. His muscles ached and his head throbbed. But the exertion had cleared his thoughts. He clenched the dagger and pressed his back against the wall outside the doorway. Raevyn's voice rose and fell in cadence, singing almost, but not quite. The light inside the room varied in intensity with her melody. Teldrin edged closer and peered into the room.

Raevyn stood with her back to him, her arms outstretched and slightly raised, her head tilted upward. She was dressed in a flowing cloud of aqua energy that whirled gently about her, floating on an arcane breeze. Her hair hung freely, twisting and turning on the same breeze.

The ring on her finger pulsed gold.

Teldrin slipped quietly into the room. Raw energy filled the room, so thick and sharp that Teldrin nearly choked on it. He looked at his dagger and saw that it, too, pulsed, joining in the flow of sorcerous power and shedding a pink light that combined with that of the ring to create flashing orange rays.

The ring.

It suddenly commanded all of his attention. Nothing else in the room existed. Nothing else mattered. Teldrin stepped closer, moving as if in a trance. This was his power. It was proper that it be his.

He shifted the dagger in his hand.

Raevyn floated on the astral breeze. The ring was a presence here. It ran a hand over her shoulder and kissed her, leaving her lips tingling with raw energy. Its heat warmed her, flowing into her, traveling through her skin and into her body.

It had been months since they had fed. She ached for more but the ring toyed with her, withholding most of the energy, letting it waft in the air around her while she digested the few droplets it allowed to pass through.

Even as her heart pounded and adrenaline carried her further into trance-state, even as her muscles quivered and soaked in warmth, even as her mind begged for more, Raevyn hated herself. It was like this every time. She could not control it, and she was afraid. Yet despite her fear, and despite the knowledge of the energy's source, something in Raevyn did not want to break free— could never bring herself to part with the ring.

Teldrin slashed downward, slicing through Raevyn's ring finger and her small finger. The room grew suddenly dark.

Pain shot through Raevyn's entire being, stabbing and exploding in every direction at once. Synapses fired. Her nerves ran with pain like molten steel.

Emptiness—a hollow vacuum like she had never felt before.

Her muscles would not respond, and Raevyn could not catch herself. She fell, screaming, her voice echoing inside her own head, reverberating along astral lines.

Then, mercifully, everything went black.

Teldrin heard Raevyn slump to the ground, and the hollow metallic sound of the ring rolling on the stone floor.

Then silence. Nothing but his own breathing. His dagger glowed strongly in the darkness, revealing Raevyn's body, two fingers missing from one hand. Oddly, there was no blood, and both stumps were healed over.

The ring lay in a corner of the room, a band of gold inlaid with jade. Teldrin walked to it and picked it up. It was warm. He put it in his pocket and moved to examine Raevyn.

He knelt over her. She was alive—her breathing shallow, but regular. Teldrin hefted his dagger; it glinted in the darkness—almost urging him on.

But killing a Lectodinian would surely result in a magewar, and Teldrin had studied enough history to know that younger wizards were always the first to die in battles between the Orders, the stronger gathering power from the weaker as they prepared for major conflicts.

Teldrin already had his quarry. He stood, sheathed his dagger, and left the room.

Teldrin returned to the clearing where three rocks were formed atop one another. It was dark and cold. His breath floated around his head like a wreath.

I can give you strength, Teldrin. I can make you the man your father never was. The voice was soft and seductive. Teldrin looked around before realizing it came from inside his own head. He reached into his pocket and pulled out the ring. It glowed blue-green in the darkness. I will give you strength—and power. Power greater than you have ever dreamed.

"You belong to my superior," Teldrin said aloud. "If I do not give it to him, I cannot become a mage."

Attruic-eb? It is not appropriate that he should be your superior. Indeed, he is nothing. We shall be his superior. As is only right. I am a master, Teldrin. I can grant your wizardry. Wear me, and we will hunt down Attruic-eb. His power will serve to bring you what is properly yours.

Teldrin held the ring between his fingers and thumb.

You are special, Teldrin. I will make you more so. You will be held in awe by your people. And why shouldn't you be? You will control anything you desire.

He studied the ring, feeling its warmth, letting it spread through his fingers and up his arms. In his mind, Teldrin saw his father, and he saw Attruic-eb.

Teldrin hardly felt himself slip the ring onto his finger.

True power was his.

Raevyn breathed deeply, truly soaking in the clean mountain air for the first time in as long as she could remember. The sky was littered with a blanket of stars, each twinkling as if to welcome her. Cricket song filled her ears.

She flexed her fingers, still unused to her missing digits. A smile crossed her face. It was worth it.

Raevyn had once been able to move this mountain if she so desired. She had been able to fly. She had made powerful men weep at her feet. But now that power was gone, and she walked down the mountain.

She was free. Free to make her own choices. Free to live her life in her own fashion. Free to show people who she really was and to choose who that person might be.

She finally had true power.

The Time of Leaving

I stood quietly in the doorway, awaiting my time. My master sat on the cold balcony in the chill wind and looked across the way, staring with unfocused eyes at the canyon walls. "Davrin?" I finally said.

He turned slowly, pulling his blanket higher over his shoulder, his fast-greying beard and the few wisps of thin hair at the sides of his head blowing faintly in sharp currents of the winter air. His eyes latched on to mine like iron talons, and the corners of his lips twitched slightly upward.

"What is it, Garrett?"

"You have a visitor," I replied.

He turned back. The canyon's walls were blood-red this time of day, stained so by the last dying rays of the sun as it set behind the castle. For a moment I thought he was going to ignore my comment. But finally, he spoke. "How long have you been apprenticed to me?"

I answered, knowing he was fully aware of the span. "Fifteen years."

"You are no longer a boy."

I cleared my throat. "I am twenty-two, no longer young."

"And your magic is now stronger than mine."

"Yes, Davrin. What is your point?"

"Why have you not left to search out your own fortune like the rest of my apprentices?"

I looked at him and considered my answer. The contour of his face stood out above the depth of the canyon. The lines chiseled in his cheeks were suddenly deep, like the shadowed crevasses that ran down the cliffs. How do I tell him that I am afraid, that I cannot rely on magic alone? How do I tell him that his strongest student cannot trust himself, that my nerves run unchecked when I think of leaving this castle? "There is more I can learn from you."

"What further lessons do you think I have to give?"

Bitter wind whistled over the exposed balcony, filling the momentary silence. "I will know when my time of leaving comes."

"My sons are already raised, Garrett. I cannot be your father."

"I do not expect that."

He nodded slowly but said nothing.

"Your visitor waits."

"I'm tired. You handle it." Using only his middle finger and forefinger, he waved me away.

"I think it would be best if you were to look

after this caller yourself."

He breathed the mountain air deeply and released the breath through his thin nostrils. "Then, by all means, let us go." Davrin rose from his chair, leaning upon a gnarled staff that stood a half a head's height above his bony pate.

I took his arm and guided him as we walked through the tower room and down the stairs.

I was never apprenticed in the formal manner. That is to say, my parents did not sell me or send me away to learn at the feet of a master of this particular trade. No. In fact, I would not know my parents if they were to announce themselves to my face. They left me to die in the streets well before I was old enough to earn my keep, while I was still merely a mouth to feed rather than an item with value for barter. Davrin took me in. He spared my life when I was tired and starving, when I weighed less than a well-fed dog and wore dirt and lice as my primary coverings. He was my savior.

He brought me home to his family, and they accepted me as one of them. Averett and Kile became my brothers. And Lorien, Davrin's wife, became my mother. Due to them, I never again knew the bitter ache of a stomach dried up in hunger. Thanks to them, I never spent another night huddled in an alleyway corner, shivering in the rain.

But life changes. Averett and Kile grew up and moved onward. And Lorien, too, moved onward, leaving the face of this earth to take residence in holier castles. After Lorien's passing, Davrin took to spending much of his time on the balcony, silently staring into the vastness of the open canyon, and withering slowly away. I felt his sorrow and I felt the emptiness to his life that she left behind.

Perhaps I remained with him for this reason. Perhaps I owed him something that I could not repay. But I knew better than to think this highly of myself. I remained because I was not ready. It was that simple, and that complex.

I would have considered my intentions further, but the visitor who awaited downstairs concerned me.

He was a slight man, this visitor. His hands were thin, his fingers sticking out of the overlarge sleeves of his tightly woven riding cloak at awkward angles, like cattails jutting out of a stagnant pond. I dare say that even a small man, such as I, could manage him well in a bare-handed fight. Yet, despite his frame, he carried himself in the way of a man familiar with power—upright and sure. His movements were bold and efficient, his language direct. And, most unsettling of all, there was something cold about the way his black eyes lit upon me as he spoke that drew my breath away, something that brought a tingle to my spine and bade me call my master to handle this case.

I wanted to tell Davrin about him. I wanted to warn him, to make sure he didn't underestimate this man who awaited our arrival. But Davrin preferred to draw his own conclusions. I would not give him these concerns until he asked for them—and his lips remained closed throughout our walk.

The visitor rose from the wicker chair as we entered the receiving room. It was a small chamber, dimly lit by globes of mage-light at each corner. Three chairs and a waist-high table filled the floor space. Shelves lined two walls, one set holding rows of leather-bound books, the other containing multicolored powders, rodent parts, and other spell catalysts.

"Good evening," Davrin said. His voice was stronger than it seemed a few minutes before. "I am sorry to have kept you waiting for so long. I am an old man, and my body does not move as fast as it once did."

"The wait was not overly long for someone who has already traveled two days."

"Any wait is too long for a visitor of mine. I did not catch your name. What may I call you?"

"Kenderick. Just call me Kenderick," our visitor replied.

Davrin's lips closed into a thin line as he moved

to stand in front of Kenderick. He analyzed our visitor as he walked; I noted the subtle changes in Davrin's expression as he scanned Kenderick's clothing, deciphered his body language, and listened to his tone of voice. Kenderick wore a brown riding cloak and highly polished, leather boots. His hands were clean and unmarked, and the hint of a golden belt buckle shone from where his cloak was unbuttoned. I could tell Davrin came to the same conclusion that I had. This man was of noble birth. And if his further study revealed the same answer as mine, Davrin would understand why I called for him.

"What do you want of me?" Davrin said.

"I have recently had a death in the family." Kenderick's voice was sharp, a razor's edge that made my nerves twinge as he spoke the word "death."

"That is always terrible to hear. You have my condolences," Davrin replied.

Kenderick nodded his head in return. "As a result, I have inherited an item that I'm told has some mystic power. But I can find no records that discuss what this power might be."

"Ah."

When Davrin went no further, Kenderick continued. "I want you to determine this item's magic and inform me of how to use it."

"Let me see the item."

Kenderick reached into a pocket and withdrew

a small velvet pouch cinched by a leather drawstring. He untied the pouch and let a small stone tumble out onto his hand. The stone was dull in the mage-light, an opaque blue several shades darker than a robin's egg. I couldn't tell from my angle, but I thought one side of the stone had been carved.

Davrin looked at it in silence for several seconds and grunted. Then he shook his head. "No," he said. And he turned to walk toward the door.

"Pardon me?" Kenderick said.

"I won't reveal the magic on your stone. I'm old, Kenderick, and tired, too. I don't have the strength to spare for the magic you request..."

I was shocked at this. Davrin had never turned a customer away. And this reason was ludicrous. Searching an object for the presence of magic was a simple spell that required little effort.

"...but my apprentice is my equal in talent. Perhaps you can convince him to help you."

The room was quiet for a moment. I looked at Kenderick and he at me. His eyebrows knit together and he raised his chin slightly, peering down his nose at me.

"Are you as good as your master says you are?"

I gave a sidelong glance at Davrin. What was he up to, I wondered? Why was he putting me in this position? It was a challenge, obviously. But what was this test's passing mark? "I can manage."

"Then will you take the task?"

"It is difficult magic," I said, using Davrin's charade to buy time.

"I have gold enough to make it worth your while."

I walked around the small table, putting it between Kenderick and myself, and turned to face him. There it was, the uneasy hood to his eyes that made me summon Davrin to this case in the first place, the sharp stare that burned my cheeks and made me want to turn away. Whatever this man's story, one thing was sure: If Kenderick had inherited the stone, his relative's death was not accidental. I glanced at Davrin and saw that his eyes had narrowed and the lines in his face had deepened.

"Bring me the stone," I said. "I will perform your spell."

Kenderick walked to the table, never removing his gaze from mine. The stone clicked against the polished wood as he laid it down. There, I could see its carving—a frontal view of an eyeball thinly etched in the surface.

I picked the stone up and rolled it between my fingertips. It was smooth, even in the area of the etching.

I placed it back on the table and went to the shelves, searching for three items. I pulled a small jar of powdered owl beak from the top shelf, and another of dried bat eyes. I dropped a pinch of the powder and two of the bat eyes into the third item, a shallow clay bowl painted in quadrants depicting each elemental power.

Returning to the table, I fished a woven mat out of the drawer and rolled it out. It made a good setting for the bowl, large enough to catch spillage, but small and plain enough to ensure the bowl a prominent status. Using both hands, I smoothed wrinkles from the cloth.

I could hear Kenderick breathing as I picked up the stone and held it over the bowl. He bent closer as I dropped the stone into the mix. He smelled of his travels, and his closeness was bothersome, making me edgy and reluctant to continue.

Davrin, too, seemed to loom closer. He stood at the perimeter of my sight, watching like a mother bird perched on a nearby tree limb.

I splayed my fingers over the edge of the bowl and focused my thoughts. The bowl's coarseness seemed to grow into me, making my fingers take on a ceramic brittleness. Then my fingers became the powder, slipping into the wrinkles of the pair of hollowed bat eyes before finding their way to the stone. It was smooth and cold, perfectly formed.

I spoke a word of magic.

Heat rose through my arm. Green light flared through my fingers, casting sudden shadows across the room, passing through the flesh of my hand to reveal an eerie view of bones and ligaments, cartilage and tendons. I drew a slow breath to calm my nerves. This was the light of power, the light of magic. But it was a light that only sorcerers such as Davrin and I could see. I struggled to avoid an outward reaction, and returned my efforts to the magic at hand. As heat traveled up my arm and crossed my chest, the full power of the stone was unveiled to me. It was intense, almost more than I could bear.

Raising my gaze, I stared at Kenderick and saw the black, malignant root of darkness that he held inside him. It festered there, twisting and churning, glistening like a mass of maggots scavenging a corpse. Kenderick's soul opened to me, and I knew his most profound desires. His dreams raged through my mind. Kenderick was a Baron, soon to rule a fiefdom. I saw his anger. I saw his distaste for the truth, his preference for quick resolution over inconvenient justice. I saw the way common people would follow him, and the bloody results if they didn't.

These visions were the stone's doing. And I was afraid.

Now that I had seen the man, could I bring myself to give Kenderick the stone's power over others? Could I allow him to see into other's lives, to steal their dreams and turn those dreams to his favor? Could I live with myself if I did? I knew the answers to these questions as I asked them, but these answers only brought a sharper edge to my anxiety. This was the fear that had brought me to call Davrin here in the first place, I realized. He should be making this decision, not me. He would know how to comport himself; I did not. He would handle this tension; I could not.

I fought the power of these thoughts, and the grotesque form that Kenderick held within. I fought for my self-control, to avoid giving Kenderick a clue to my findings. As I withdrew from the stone, the images trickled away, and I concentrated on regular breathing. I moved through the powder and the bowl, quieting my heartbeat and struggling to overcome the nervous energy that came with knowing I would soon have to confront my fears.

Finally, I returned to my normal self, and the spell's energy faded. I looked at Kenderick. Even without the stone's magic, I could see the writhing darkness in his pupils.

"Well?" he said.

I swallowed and shook my head, wondering if my voice would waver. "There is no magic on this stone."

Kenderick paused for a moment. "None?"

"None," I lied again.

A sigh of resignation escaped Kenderick's lips. I glanced at my master and saw a thin smile on his face and a glimmer in his eye.

I stood quietly in the doorway, awaiting my time.

Davrin sat on the cold balcony in the chill wind and looked across the way, staring with unfocused eyes at the canyon walls. Those walls were dull brown this time of the morning, waiting for the sun to rise over the highest crests.

I didn't know how to proceed. I was here to tell Davrin that I was prepared to leave, that his work was complete. But despite his earlier prodding and my eagerness to make my leaving, I suddenly found the words difficult.

"Davrin?" I finally said.

"We lived here because Lorien loved these cliffs," he said before I could say more.

"They are beautiful," I replied. "Almost as breathtaking as she was."

He turned and looked at me. His frail body and his shrunken face seemed almost hollow, lifeless. But his eyes flared with a passion sparked by the mention of Lorien's beauty.

"She was my life," he said.

He turned back to the canyon walls. For a moment I thought he had forgotten about me.

Thoughts tumbled through my mind, colliding with each other and mixing themselves up. My heart pounded against my breast. My throat choked. I wanted to talk to him. I wanted to tell him what his guidance had meant to me, to thank him for giving me a life. There was so much I wanted to say.

But as these words stuck in my throat, a memory wedged its way in. I remembered my youthful anticipation as I would wait in the castle for his return from distant lands, the warm look on his face as he burst through the doorway, and the smell of the woods on his hands and clothes when he greeted me with hugs of the same fervor as those he had for Averett and Kile.

What would my life have been without Davrin? Where would I have been without Lorien?

I gazed at him. His head shook with more than the cold. His lips were dry and creased, showing no signs of having been treated with the oils that Lorien would have made him apply. His hair blew about his uncovered head.

A new thought managed to struggle through my own selfish concerns. One so disturbing that it caught my breath and drew me harshly back into reality.

Davrin had never been alone before.

"When are you leaving?" he asked.

I swallowed and cleared my throat. There was only one answer to this question. My time of leaving would come when Davrin's came, and this was not it. "I am not ready yet."

He grimaced. "I have nothing more for you, Garrett. You should go and live your life. Leave an old man in peace."

"No, I disagree. There is much more I can learn from you."

Davrin pursed his lips.

I walked to his chair and knelt beside him, warming his cold hand in mine. "I'll make our breakfast in a moment. But first, tell me about when you first met Lorien."

He sat in silence for a moment, staring at the cliffs. Then he began to speak. As he described their first meeting, the sun crested the far ridge of the canyon. I raised my free hand and shielded my eyes, squinting into the light of a new day.

Acknowledgments

I have an eclectic bunch to thank for this volume.

My first thank you goes out to Louise Rowder, Imp-extraordinaire, whose very deftly crafted critique of an early draft of "The Time of Leaving" helped make it what it is. Thanks, also, to Laura Resnick, for whom "A Gathering of Bones" would not exist. Thanks to Kent Brewster for being the first to point out a typo in "Ties That Bind." It's amazing what a difference the letter "R" can make, eh? Needless to say, that typo no longer exists. I want to thank Anthony Bryant, for picking "True Power" out of the slush at *Dragon*, and finally, Barbara Young, also of *Dragon*, for sending me a remarkably wonderful note as she accepted the piece.

But above all others I need to thank Lisa. You are, and will always be, the person who makes me who I am.

About Ron Collins

Ron Collins is an Amazon best-selling Dark Fantasy author who writes across the spectrum of speculative fiction.

His fantasy series *Saga of the God-Touched Mage* reached #1 on Amazon's bestselling dark fantasy list in the UK, #2 in the US. His short fiction has received a Writers of the Future prize and a CompuServe HOMer Award, and his short story "The White Game" was nominated for the Short Mystery Fiction Society's 2016 Derringer Award.

He has contributed a hundred or so short stories to *Analog*, *Asimov's*, Fiction River Anthology Series, and several other professional magazines and anthologies.

- - -

www.typosphere.com | Twitter: @roncollins13

- - -

Sign up for Ron's Newsletter and get a free ebook!
http://www.typosphere.com/newsletter

www.ingramcontent.com/pod-product-compliance
Lightning Source LLC
Chambersburg PA
CBHW070517200726
48293CB00007B/2575